Shamrock Sean
and the Bird's Nest

Brian Gogarty

Illustrated by Roxanne Burchartz
of The Cartoon Saloon

THE O'BRIEN PRESS
DUBLIN

For my wife, Eileen, and children Christine,
Nuala and Ryan, because they believe ...

First published 2007 by The O'Brien Press Ltd.
12 Terenure Road East, Rathgar, Dublin 6, Ireland.
Tel: +353 1 4923333; Fax: +353 1 4922777
E-mail: books@obrien.ie
Website: www.obrien.ie
Reprinted 2010.

ISBN: 978-0-86278-969-5

British Library Cataloguing-in-Publication Data
Gogarty, Brian
Shamrock Sean and the bird's nest
1. Shamrock Sean (Fictitious character) - Pictorial works -Juvenile fiction
2. Birds - Infancy - Pictorial works - Juvenile fiction
3. Children's stories - Pictorial works
I. Title
823.9'2[J]

2 3 4 5 6
10 11 12 13

The O'Brien Press receives assistance from

the arts
council
schomhairle
ealaíon

Editing, typesetting and design: The O'Brien Press Ltd
Printing: Leo Paper Products Ltd

These are the adventures of a lively leprechaun,

He's from the west of Ireland, his name is Shamrock Sean.

He has a little bushy beard, his hair is thick and grey.

He's older than the Blarney Stone if he's a single day.

He loves to eat potatoes – boiled or mashed or roast,

But cabbage mixed with bacon is what he loves the most.

He lives inside a toadstool, beneath a tree of oak,

And if you wander Knock-Na-Shee you might

see his chimney smoke.

One day in the springtime

Shamrock Sean worked near the hedge.

Digging in his garden,

He was planting greens and veg.

He leant upon his garden spade

To have a little rest,

And from the corner of his eye

He spied a small bird's nest.

He climbed between the branches

And stood upon one leg.

There, hidden down inside the nest,

He saw a single egg.

By a miracle of nature

The egg began to crack,

It made him lose his balance,

And he stumbled and fell back.

Just then the mother bird appeared

And said, 'What did you do?

My little egg's not due to hatch

For another day or two.'

Sean said, 'I just stood on the branch

To get a better view.

I didn't touch your little egg,

Honestly, it's true.'

'I must find worms,' said mother bird,

'But since he's newly born,

I can't go off in search of food

And leave him on his own.'

'I've got it! Don't you worry,'

responded Shamrock Sean.

'You stay here and leave the food

To this here Leprechaun.'

So Sean ran to his garden

Where the soil was freshly tilled.

He collected worms in handfuls

'Till a bucket load was filled.

He came back to the hungry chick

And said, 'I've worms galore.

If there's not enough to feed him,

I can get a whole lot more.'

'Thank you, Sean, you're very kind,'

the mother bird then said.

And she lifted up a wing

To pat him gently on the head.

'I thought that leprechauns were mean,

Or so I have been told.

But now I know it isn't true –

you're worth your weight in gold.'